For Ellie —J.A.
For Lukas —A.M.

Text copyright © 2020 by Jennifer Adams
Illustrations copyright © 2020 by Alea Marley
Published by Roaring Brook Press
Roaring Brook Press is a division of Holtzbrinck Publishing Holdings Limited Partnership
120 Broadway, New York, NY 10271
mackids.com

Library of Congress Control Number: 2019948840

ISBN: 978-1-250-31005-7

Our books may be purchased in bulk for promotional, educational, or business use. Please contact your local
bookseller or the Macmillan Corporate and Premium Sales Department at (800) 221-7945 ext. 5442 or by
email at MacmillanSpecialMarkets@macmillan.com.

First edition, 2020
Book design by Monique Sterling
Printed in China by Hung Hing Off-set Printing Co. Ltd.,
Heshan City, Guangdong Province

1 3 5 7 9 10 8 6 4 2

Goodnight,
LITTLE SUPERHERO

BY Jennifer Adams

ILLUSTRATED BY

Alea Marley

Roaring Brook Press

New York

It's time for bed,
little superhero.

Super
City

Time to tell us all *goodnight.*

Head back home, pack up your gear,

then fly to bed and dim the light.

Goodnight, *cape*, and goodnight, *sidekick*.

Goodnight, *mask* **and** *badge* **and** *tights.*

Goodnight, world outside your window.

You are safe and sound tonight.

Goodnight, bad guys.
Goodnight, good guys.

It won't be long before
you meet.

You've been brave and bold all day,

but even heroes go to sleep.

Now let's rest your superpowers,

so when you need them

they'll be strong.

You can save the world tomorrow.

Tonight, you're home where you belong.